N/A

BARNEY BACKHOE
AND THE
BIG CITY DIG

By Susan Knopf · Illustrated by Jerry Zimmerman

RUNNING PRESS
KIDS
PHILADELPHIA·LONDON

Library of Congress Control Number: 2006923193

ISBN-13: 978-0-7624-2659-1
ISBN-10: 0-7624-2659-4

This book may be ordered by mail from the publisher.
Please include $2.50 for postage and handling.
But try your bookstore first!

Published by Running Press Kids, an imprint of
Running Press Book Publishers
125 South Twenty-Second Street
Philadelphia, Pennsylvania 19103-4399

Created and produced by Parachute Press.
Parachute Publishing, L.L.C.
156 Fifth Avenue
New York, New York 10010

Visit us on the web!
www.runningpress.com

"Look, everyone!" Barney Backhoe said to his friends. "I have big news. There's an important job for us to do in the city. Let's go help build a skyscraper!"

"That sounds great!" said Eddie Excavator. "Let's go right now!"

"But we have to finish this playground first," said Grady Grader.

"Why don't you go ahead, Barney?" Luke Loader suggested. "You're fast, and you can do two things at once."

"We'll finish the playground and then meet you at the big city dig," Danny Dozer added.

Barney zoomed down the road to the city. He couldn't wait to get to the big dig.

Barney passed a pipe yard, a place where pipes are stored. Oh, no! Some of the pipes had rolled into the road.

I can help, Barney thought. First he lifted the bigger pipes with his loader shovel. Then he scooped up the smaller pipes with his backhoe bucket.

Barney continued down the road. Soon he reached the big city! He looked up at the tall buildings.

Oh, no! A builder was waving his arms for help. The man's ladders had fallen to the ground. He couldn't get up or down to finish his job.

Max's
Cafe

I can help, Barney thought. He lifted the ladders into place. *Now the builder can finish his job.*

"I have had a very busy day, and I haven't even gotten to the big dig yet!" Barney said as he hurried along. . . .

. . . but then he stopped.

Oh, no! There was a great big hole in the middle of the road. Barney saw a truck carrying lots of glass windows. If the truck tried to drive over that hole, the windows would break!

GLASS

BIG CITY DIG

Hotel

JOHN DEERE

I can help, Barney thought. He scooped up some gravel and filled the hole. *Now the truck can get through.* Then Barney zoomed off to the big city dig.

Finally Barney arrived at the construction site. His friends were already there. They were hard at work. "I've had a busy day!" Barney said. "First I stacked pipes, then I lifted two tall ladders, and finally I filled a giant hole in the road!"

Barney looked at the big dig. The work was almost finished. "But I didn't help you very much on the big city dig," he said to his friends sadly.

BIG CITY DIG

"Yes, you did!" said Eddie Excavator. "You helped us by picking up the pipes at the pipe yard . . . and here they are!"

Barney dug a long hole, and Eddie placed the pipes into the hole.

Next Barney lifted some beams up to the builder.

"You also helped us by picking up the ladders so the builder could get to his next job—right here!" Danny said.

"And you helped us by filling in the hole in the road so the truck with the windows could get past," said Luke. "And here they are!"

Barney and Luke carried the windows very carefully so they wouldn't break.

Soon the new buildings were finished! The mayor came to celebrate. Everyone cheered for Barney Backhoe and his friends.

"We did it!" Barney said to his friends. "Thanks for helping with the big city dig!"

"We couldn't have done it without you, Barney!" said Danny Dozer.

DID YOU KNOW . . . ?

Heavy blade

Tough crawlers

Danny Dozer

- Has a big blade for pushing rocks and dirt.
- Can dig up roots and tree stumps to clear the land.
- Has a tough engine under the hood.
- Has crawlers instead of wheels to help climb steep, rough paths.

Barney Backhoe

- Has two buckets—one on each end!
- Can dig a hole with his backhoe bucket.
- Can scoop, carry, and pour dirt with his front loader bucket.
- Can lift building materials up high, to where they're needed.

Backhoe bucket

Loader bucket

Strong boom

Long arm

Huge crawlers

Eddie Excavator

- Can reach far down into a hole to dig deeply.
- Has crawlers to help him move easily on rocky surfaces.
- Can turn his body in all directions without moving his crawlers.
- Has a sharp edge on his bucket for breaking up hard ground.

DID YOU KNOW . . . ?

Large shovel

JOHN DEERE

Very big wheels

Grady Grader

- Can clear and smooth out the ground to help build roads.
- Has a long, sharp blade that moves around in a circle.
- Has two wheels in front of his blade, and four wheels behind it.

Luke Loader

- Has a huge bucket for carrying lots of dirt and rocks.
- Can lift a load of dirt way up high to pour it into a dump truck.
- Can use a forklift to carry building supplies.

JOHN DEERE

Six wheels   Sharp blade